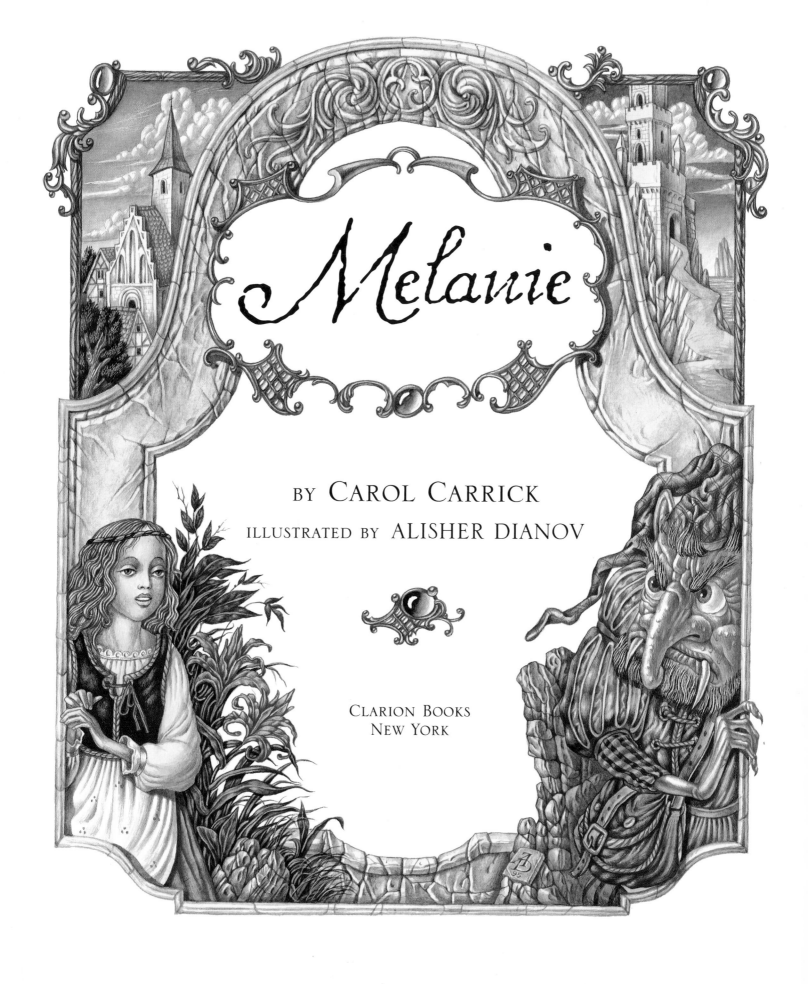

Melanie

BY CAROL CARRICK

ILLUSTRATED BY ALISHER DIANOV

CLARION BOOKS
NEW YORK

Clarion Books
a Houghton Mifflin Company imprint
215 Park Avenue South, New York, NY 10003
Text copyright © 1996 by Carol Carrick
Illustrations copyright © 1996 by Alisher Dianov

The illustrations for this book were executed in watercolor.
The text is set in 16/19-point Meridien.

For information about this and other Houghton Mifflin
trade and reference books and multimedia products,
visit The Bookstore at Houghton Mifflin on the World Wide Web
at (http://www.hmco.com/trade/).

Printed in Singapore.

Library of Congress Cataloging-in-Publication Data

Carrick, Carol.
Melanie / by Carol Carrick ; illustrated by Alisher Dianov.
p. cm.
Summary: When her grandfather goes in search of one who can heal her
of her blindness and fails to return, Melanie follows
and rescues him from a hideous troll.
ISBN 0-395-66555-8
[1. Trolls—Fiction. 2. Grandfathers—Fiction. 3. Blind—Fiction.
4. Physically handicapped—Fiction.] I. Dianov, Alisher, ill. II. Title.
PZ7.C2344Me 1996
[E]—dc20   94-15592
CIP
AC

TWP 10 9 8 7 6 5 4 3 2 1

For Mary Coles
—C.C.

For my great friends
Vladimir V. and Valery M.
and also in memory of my father
—A.D.

$\mathcal{T}$HERE ONCE WAS A BLIND GIRL NAMED MELANIE, who was as lovely as her name. Each morning she led her small flock of sheep to the hills where the sweet grass grew. She knew each animal by its voice and the sheep trusted her gentleness. Even when she sheared their fleece, they did not struggle.

At sunset, Grandfather rang a bell. By following its sound, Melanie drove the sheep back down the hill and shut them in the barn where they would be safe.

"Here, sit by the fire," the old man would say to the girl, "and warm your hands on this bowl of soup." After supper, while Melanie spun the fleece into yarn, she would ask him to tell her a story.

"Three days' journey from here," said Grandfather one night, "there lies a forest of trees so tall that they hide the sun. Many travelers from this town have lost their way in the Dark Forest. Others are eaten by wild animals that prowl through its endless night."

Hearing this, Melanie shuddered.

"There is a bridge at the end of the forest," said Grandfather, "which leads to the North Kingdom. Under it lurks an ugly troll. He uses his magic to rob all who cross over by changing them into gulls. The gulls circle the bridge, crying out to the troll, but the troll ignores them. No one but the gulls knows how the evil spell works," said Grandfather, finishing his story. "But gulls cannot speak."

Soon the old man dozed, and his candle sputtered and went out. But Melanie worked far into the night, weaving her yarn into cloth while the enchanted birds drifted across her mind.

Each week on market day Grandfather walked to town, making his way past storytellers, past the lace sellers and the fragrant pie and sausage stalls to his space next to the harness maker. There he sold Melanie's cloth to the town's wealthy women to make into fine clothing. Because Grandfather loved Melanie dearly, he worried—what would become of her when he died?

One day a lace seller spoke of a healer who lived beyond the Dark Forest. She said he cured by the touch of his hand. Perhaps he could give Melanie sight.

When Grandfather told Melanie of the healer, she danced with excitement. "You must take me to him," she said.

But the old man was afraid for her. Travel was dangerous in those times. This would be a hard trip, even for one who could see.

"Please, Grandfather!" The girl's eyes were shining. "How wonderful it would be to see your face and to see the candle-light!"

How could he refuse her? "Child," he said, stroking her cheek, "I will find the healer and bring him to you."

Then Melanie recalled her grandfather's story about the wild animals in the forest and the evil troll who guarded the bridge. She was sorry now that she had made him promise to go.

"Don't worry," he comforted her. "I will be back before the next market day." Taking what money they had, he kissed her good-bye.

10

All the while Grandfather was gone, Melanie sat on the hillside tending her flock. As she waited, she imagined how it would be to see the wind brushing the grass, to see the flowers nodding in the sun and the young lambs gamboling on the hill. At the end of the day, though Grandfather was not there to guide her home, she followed the warmth of the setting sun down the hill.

At first Melanie was not anxious. But when market day came and Grandfather did not, she feared something had happened to him. Then another market day passed without news. Melanie was haunted by thoughts of the wicked troll who changed travelers into birds. Even the crows on the hillside seemed to cry with Grandfather's voice. "Free me! Set me free!" they cawed.

By the third market day Melanie made up her mind. Grandfather had gone on this journey for her. Now she must find and help him. Although she feared for her sheep, she left them untended and set out for the troll's bridge. All she took with her was her shepherd's staff and a basket full of bread and cheese. She managed to keep heading north by feeling the morning sun on her right shoulder and the setting sun on her left.

By the end of the first day her basket was empty. At night she huddled by the side of the road where the smell of grass reminded her of her sheep. *Dear ones,* she thought, *I pray you are safe without me. Are you letting the wise ewe with the ragged ear lead? And are the lambs keeping close by?* Feeling miserable, she wished for their warmth to snuggle against and the company of their voices.

On the next day Melanie set out before the sun was high. Soon she was hot and dusty. Her throat felt so dry she could hardly swallow. Growing tired, she began to doubt. Would she ever reach the North Kingdom?

When she awoke the next morning the ground was soaked with dew and the perfume of crushed strawberries. Eagerly she combed the wild berries from the grass, licking their sweetness from her fingers.

On the third day the road dwindled to a path so narrow she could touch trees on both sides with her outstretched fingers. Few travelers ever dared to enter the Dark Forest.

At first the shade was refreshing. Melanie heard the sound of water where a brook ran near the path, and she knelt gratefully and drank. Birds sang in the canopy above. Leaves rustled. Then fear crept in with the chill. If the trees hid the warmth of the sun, how would she find her way north?

A squirrel scolded. She heard him spiral up a tree. Melanie reached out to feel the bark. Touching moss, she remembered— moss was said to grow on the north side of trees. From time to time she would check for moss.

A dry branch snapped. She was startled. A heavy tread tramped down a thicket. With a crash, something large burst onto the path. It had an odor so strong she could smell it even at a distance. A bear?

Her heart was pounding. *Don't be afraid,* she told herself. *Keep walking. The bear will go its own way.*

She tried to think of Grandfather. How happy they would be when she found him! At last, when she heard only the faint stirring of leaves, she dropped with weariness and slept.

Melanie's sleep was not peaceful. In her dreams she tried to catch up with the white birds, but they kept drifting away. Grandfather's voice called out to her—*Melanie!*—but the trees drew close to hold her back.

A loud bellow woke her. At first it was frightening, but then she listened. She heard stamping hooves, the rattle of antlers, and the sound of thrashing. *An elk must be caught in some brambles*, she thought. With each toss of his head he sounded more ensnared.

Melanie stood up and approached the frantic beast, soothing him by talking calmly, the way she quieted her sheep. When the elk grew silent, she patiently untangled him. The briars were sharp, but years of hard work had toughened her hands.

Melanie knew that elks roam north in the spring. She could follow him, but she would not be able to keep up. So before he shook himself free, she leaped upon his back and gripped the thick fur of his ruff.

With a surprised snort, the elk scrambled to his knees and fled through the forest. Low branches tore at Melanie's hair. She clung desperately to the elk, pressing her face against his neck.

Soon the wind carried a taste of the sea. Sensing danger, the elk stopped. Melanie urged him on but he would not move. When she slid from his back, he ran off.

From a distance came the faint cries of gulls. Melanie raised her head and listened. With the wind in her face, she staggered toward the sea. She had lost her shepherd's staff and her feet sank deep in the sand.

The birds sounded closer, mournful and wailing as they had in her dreams. Could the troll truly enchant people, turning them into birds? If so, one of these might be Grandfather.

Now the slap of waves had a hollow sound, the way they would echo under the troll's bridge. Melanie took a deep breath. What would she do if he caught her? She had no gold to bargain with.

Cautiously, she felt for the planks with her bare feet and started across the long bridge. One wrong step and she could topple off and fall into the sea.

A great cry went up when the gulls saw her. They flew at Melanie, pulling her hair, trying to drive her away.

"Grandfather!" she called out, shielding her face with her arms. "Are you there?"

The troll was on the far shore, counting his stolen gold. Trusting no one, he kept it in a sack around his neck. He looked up when he heard the birds' alarm and saw the small figure crossing his bridge.

Melanie felt the thud of feet pounding toward her. As the noise came closer she smelled something like rotting meat, the terrible stench of troll.

"Halt!" the troll shouted, even though she had already stopped—she was paralyzed with fear. "Hand over your gold."

"But I have none," said Melanie.

It was a good thing she could not see his face or she might have fainted.

The troll scowled. It made him seem even more horrible.

"Then you are under my spell," he said. "For all who are frightened by my face are changed at once into birds."

Melanie let out a sigh of relief. Planting her feet wide, she said, "Then I am *not* under your spell."

"Look at me," the troll growled, not knowing she was blind. "Tell me I am not frightening."

Melanie almost smiled.

"You don't look frightening to me," she said. "And you never will."

The troll flew into a rage. With a great effort, he bulged his bloodshot eyes and ground his ragged teeth. "*Now* tell me I don't look frightening."

Melanie laughed.

"Ha!" snarled the troll, losing his temper, "I'll teach you to laugh at me." And he grabbed Melanie by the arms. She kicked and thrashed, biting the troll's hand, but he would not release her.

The birds dived at the troll. As the girl struggled, they beat him with their wings. Still he would not let her go. Then the old gull with the whitest head pecked at the troll's eyes.

With a cry of rage, the troll backed away and fell into the sea, taking Melanie with him.

They sank down, down beneath the waves. Melanie tried to pull free of the troll, but he clutched her tightly until they both lost consciousness. Weighted by his gold, the troll sank to the bottom and drowned, but Melanie floated free.

Now that the troll was dead, the air filled with feathers as the birds drifted gently to earth and changed back into people. The bird with the whitest head was Grandfather.

Light as a flower, Melanie rose to the surface. The troll's prisoners pulled her from the sea and laid her on a soft carpet of feathers. Grandfather held her in his arms. She was as still and as cold as marble until his tears warmed her back to life.

When all the people Melanie had set free saw that she was alive, they clapped and cheered. They lifted her and Grandfather onto the troll's own horse and led them safely home.

As they entered the town gates there was a great celebration with music and feasting. The mayor made a speech and presented a sack of gold to the brave girl who had rescued the towns-people's loved ones and rid them of the troll.

Still Grandfather was troubled. "Child," he said, "my great wish was to bring you sight. I searched and searched only to find that there was no healer, merely a wicked troll."

But Melanie was not discouraged. "I found you," she said. "And if I had been able to see the troll, I, too, would have been changed into a bird."

Arm in arm they walked home, where Melanie's sheep were waiting. Soon she was roaming with them on the grassy hills while Grandfather slept peacefully in the sun.